THE TIME WARP TRIO series

THE TIME WARP TRIO

Oh Say,
I Can't See

by Jon Scieszka

illustrated by Adam McCauley

VIKING

VIKING
Published by Penguin Group
Penguin Young Readers Group, 345 Hudson Street, New York, New York 10014, U.S.A.
Penguin Group (Canada), 90 Eglinton Avenue East, Suite 700, Toronto, Ontario,
Canada M4P 2Y3 (a division of Pearson Penguin Canada Inc.)
Penguin Books Ltd, 80 Strand, London WC2R 0RL, England
Penguin Ireland, 25 St Stephen's Green, Dublin 2, Ireland (a division of Penguin Books Ltd)
Penguin Group (Australia), 250 Camberwell Road, Camberwell, Victoria 3124, Australia
(a division of Pearson Australia Group Pty Ltd)
Penguin Books India Pvt Ltd, 11 Community Centre, Panchsheel Park, New Delhi - 110 017, India
Penguin Group (NZ), Cnr Airborne and Rosedale Roads, Albany, Auckland 1310,
New Zealand (a division of Pearson New Zealand Ltd)
Penguin Books (South Africa) (Pty) Ltd, 24 Sturdee Avenue, Rosebank,
Johannesburg 2196, South Africa

Penguin Books Ltd, Registered Offices: 80 Strand, London WC2R 0RL, England

First published in 2005 by Viking, a division of Penguin Young Readers Group

1 3 5 7 9 10 8 6 4 2

Text copyright © Jon Scieszka, 2005
Illustrations copyright © Penguin Group (USA) Inc., 2005
Illustrations by Adam McCauley
All rights reserved

LIBRARY OF CONGRESS CATALOGING-IN-PUBLICATION DATA
Scieszka, Jon.
Oh say, I can't see / by Jon Scieszka ; illustrated by Adam McCauley.
p. cm. — (Time warp trio)
Summary: After arriving in Pennsylvania during the winter of 1776, time
travelers Joe, Fred, and Samantha inspire General George Washington, "the
man on the one dollar bill," to carry out a surprise attack on Hessian troops
in Trenton, New Jersey, that will change the course of the Revolutionary War.
ISBN 0-670-06025-9 (hardcover)
[1. Time travel—Fiction. 2. Trenton, Battle of, Trenton, N.J., 1776—Fiction.
3. United States—History—Revolution, 1775–1783—Campaigns—Fiction.
4. Washington, George, 1732–1799—Fiction. 5. Humorous stories.]
I. Title: Oh say, I cannot see. II. McCauley, Adam, ill. III. Title.
PZ7.S41267Oh 2005
[Fic]—dc22
2005017737

Printed in U.S.A.
Set in Sabon

To the George Washington
in all of us

J. S.

To Clement and Esmeralda,
future revolutionaries

A. M.

ONE

"**B**ad cat," said Samantha. "Very bad cat. Bad, bad, bad . . . Joe? Bad . . . Fred?"

Samantha—and we knew it had to be Samantha because no one else has that same crazy hair—Samantha stopped looking under a snow-covered bush and stared at us.

"Joe and Fred, what are you guys doing here?"

Fred and I looked around. We didn't even know where "here" was. We were standing in the middle of a small group of trees. Down a hill a good-sized river flowed by. The ground was covered with snow. Fred still held the snowball he had just made on my street in Brooklyn. But this definitely wasn't Brooklyn. And since we were looking at Sam's great-granddaughter from one hundred years in the future, I had a bad feeling this wasn't the twenty-first century either.

"We were just going to ask you the same thing," I said.

"Yeah," said Fred. He pegged his snowball. It exploded against a tree. "Two seconds ago we were at home bombing each other with snowballs. Now we're out in the boonies. What gives?"

Samantha suddenly got very busy fixing the edge of her silver coat. She mumbled, "Well, *The Book* must have been set on Automatic Three-Warp. We just have to find my cat."

Samantha started walking around the trees calling, "Here, Rivets. Here, kitty kitty."

I heard what she said, but I didn't want to believe it. "Samantha, did you just say *The Book*?"

"Here, kitty kitty," said Samantha.

"Oh man," said Fred. He made another snowball. "Don't tell me you warped us somewhere crazy the day before Christmas just to help find your cat."

"Here, kitty kitty," said Samantha.

"Samantha!" I yelled.

Fred threw his snowball at her. It should have bounced off her back. But it just kind of weirdly disappeared against the silvery material of her coat.

"Stop with the kitty stuff," I said. "And tell us where and when and why we are here."

Samantha looked thoughtful for a second. She pushed her glasses up on her nose exactly the same way Sam does. "You don't have to get all snervely, you know. It's really quite simple. The snow. The river. We are in Pennsylvania, Christmas Eve, seventeen seventy-six, the day before Washington crosses the Delaware."

"Oh great," I said. I threw my own snowball and exploded it on a nearby tree. "That explains where and when perfectly. But *why* exactly are *we* here?"

Samantha twirled one of her many ponytails. "Well, it's actually because um . . . my homework project . . . I mean Rivets, my cat . . . that is, I borrowed *The Book* from Joanie—"

"And I thought Sam gave spastic answers," said Fred. "Spit it out."

Samantha gave Fred a nasty look. "We are here because my homework ate my cat."

Fred and I thought about this for a second. Samantha looked so serious. We cracked up.

"That is the worst excuse I have ever heard," said Fred.

"And Fred should know," I said. "He is the master of the bad excuse."

"Your homework ate your cat," said Fred. "Of course." Fred laughed again.

"It's true," said Samantha. She tried to make a snowball and throw it at Fred. But she ended up just spraying a handful of snow in his general direction. Then all in one breath she said, "I'm sure you old-timers won't understand the technical details, but I was transferring my holo-report on George Washington crossing the Delaware when my cat Rivets, and yes I know she has some problems, her model was never upgraded, had an accident. See I borrowed *The Book* from Joanie because I was a little late with my assignment. And of course the one way to make time is to warp back in time. And I thought I could also get some good information for my report directly from General Washington, or at least get some real details about the place and time, you know. But anyhow—to make a long story short—Rivets jumped through the holo-report, erased it, and accidentally leaked on *The Book,* which triggered the Automatic Three-Warp that it's usually set on, and since I was the only one nearby, it included you two to make three, understand?"

Fred and I stood there with our mouths hanging open.

"Huh?" said Fred.

"Right," I said. I didn't understand half of what she said, but I wasn't going to tell her that.

The sinking winter sun barely peeked through the clouds. It was getting colder. I didn't remember much about George Washington crossing the Delaware. There is that famous picture of him standing up in a boat. And there is a lot of ice in a river and guys with guns. But I do know that whenever we time warp, we manage to get in trouble. This did not sound good.

"So where is *The Book*? And how do we warp out of here?" I said.

"Oh, that's easy," said Samantha. "I programmed Rivets to always search out *The Book*. We find Rivets, we find *The Book*."

"Ha!" said Fred. He heaved another snowball high over the trees. "A broken robot cat is going to warp us home?"

The snowball disappeared over a hill. We heard it land with a thud. Then we heard a sound we weren't expecting—the sound of an angry voice.

"*Hey!* It came from over there."

Three ragged-looking soldiers with long rifles charged over the top of the hill and spotted us.

"Oh no," I said.

"Freeze right there, spies," they said.

For once in all our time warp history, it wasn't our fault. Really. But that didn't seem to matter to the guys pointing their rifles at us.

We were about to become history.

All because Samantha's homework ate her cat.

TWO

We knew it couldn't be as easy as finding a cat.

You knew it couldn't be as easy as finding a cat.

Somehow, time warping is never as easy as you might hope.

But before George Washington's men string us up as spies, I'd like to explain how we got into this mess.

I'd like to, but I can't.

The truth is, I have no idea how we got to 1776 just before Washington crossed the Delaware. But maybe I can tell you the basics and what Samantha told us. Then you're on your own.

See, I think of myself as a pretty regular kid. I live in a pretty regular neighborhood in Brooklyn. I go to a pretty regular school. And I have two pretty regular best friends, Fred and Sam.

I guess the part that's not so regular is this book

I got from my uncle Joe for my birthday. I don't know quite how to put it, but somehow this book can warp time and space. And somehow this book has sent Fred and Sam and me back to the Stone Age, over to 1600s Japan to fight samurai warriors, back to meet the pharaoh in Egypt, and into the future to meet our own great-granddaughters.

So much for regular.

We've gotten into trouble all over history because it's kind of hard to tell how *The Book* works exactly. Sometimes a word or poem triggers the time warping. Sometimes it's a picture or a symbol.

The one thing we have found for sure is that after we time warp, the only way to warp back home safely is to find *The Book*. Which is always way easier to say than it is to do.

So this time, Fred and I were on the street outside my house. Sam was off visiting his grandma in Florida. It was the day before Christmas. Snowing like crazy. Vacation. Perfect.

I ducked behind a tree just in time. Fred's snowball popped against the tree trunk. I jumped out with two snowballs and launched my favorite sneak attack. It works almost every time. I threw a high soft lob. Fred looked up to dodge it. Then I pitched a fastball right at him. He was still watching the lob when the fastball nailed him in the chest.

"Arrrgh," said Fred. He scooped up his own snowball. He cocked his arm to throw it. And then without warning—without us touching *The Book*, going anywhere near *The Book*, or even thinking about *The Book*—the swirling white snow turned to swirling green time-warping mist.

And we were gone.

For the first and maybe only time ever, it wasn't our fault.

I know we say that all the time. But this time it was really true.

So what happened?

I'll let Samantha explain it to you . . . and to the soldiers about to do us in.

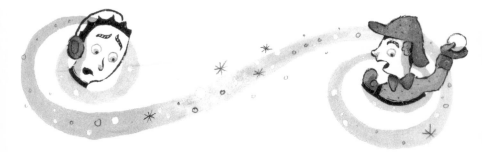

THREE

The three soldiers backed us against a tree, their rifles pointed at our chests. They didn't look at all like those pictures of soldiers you usually see in the history books. No uniforms. No fancy boots. Their clothes and guns looked all beat-up and dirty.

They wore long fringed shirts almost down to their knees, cloth wrapped around their legs, and fur caps. They looked young and scrawny.

"These are the guys who beat the redcoats and started our country?" said Fred.

They may have been wearing rags, but all three had a hard look in their eyes.

"Let's not make the nice men with guns mad, Fred," I said. I was trying to remember anything I could about Washington and his soldiers crossing the Delaware. All I could remember was that painting. I wished Sam were with us.

11

"What are you three doing out here?" asked the biggest soldier. "Spying on the generals?" He pointed his long rifle up at my forehead.

"Spies? Us?" I said. "Heck no. We're regular Americans just like you. Glad to be here helping Washington cross the Delaware, whites of their eyes, don't tread on me. . . ."

"See?" said the second soldier to the third. "I told you."

"Yeah," said Fred. "We're here to help with the rockets' red glare, bombs bursting in air, and all that."

"That was the Civil War, Fred," said Samantha.

"No way, that's 'The Star Spangled Banner,'" said Fred.

"Never mind," said Samantha.

"You were right, Ethan," said the third soldier. "They're spies all right. Kind of small for Hessians. But them are dang strange boots and hunting shirts."

Samantha's silver coat did look a little strange. But Fred and I were just wearing our regular winter coats and boots.

"My mom made me wear the boots because it was snowing," I said.

"Let's shoot 'em," said the soldier.

"Let's not," said Fred. "We don't even know what a Hessian is . . . do we?"

"Uh, Samantha," I said. "This is where Sam usually comes up with a very smart

13

piece of history or science or math, and impresses people so much that they don't kill us. Could you help us out here?"

Samantha jumped from one foot to another, squinting one eye and squeezing one edge of her glasses.

"Oooh, this will be perfect for the intro." She squeezed her glasses again. "One more. And could you in the middle there—hold your rifle gun thingy up just a bit higher? That's it. Now look mean, desperate, hungry."

The soldiers already looked mean, desperate, hungry.

"That is so perfecto," said Samantha. "I am going to ace this project." She spoke into her wristband like she was an announcer for the Discovery Channel or something. "Christmas Eve, seventeen seventy-six. Washington's men are mean, desperate, hungry. The fate of this young country is in their hands."

Now the soldiers looked mean, desperate, hungry, and confused.

"Samantha," I said. "What are you doing?"

"Just saving a bit of vid." She tapped her glasses. "I also found in my History Files that these guys are probably from New Hampshire. Some of Johnny Stark's men."

"These little buggers know way too much," said the leader. "They is definitely Hessian spies."

"No way," said Fred. "We are definitely not Hessian spies. Look at my hat. It says 'Made in the U.S.A.'"

Fred showed the New Hampshire boys his hat. They were not impressed.

Samantha kept tapping her glasses.

"Time for a little magic, Joe," said Fred. "Get us out of here."

I looked around for any sign of Samantha's cat and *The Book*. Nothing but snow. Nowhere to run but the river. I racked my brain for a magic trick. This didn't look like a crowd that would fall for the two snowball trick.

"Samantha, don't you have any valuable information our friends might need us to tell General Washington—alive and in person?"

Samantha looked cross-eyed staring up into one corner of her glasses. "Bunker Hill . . . Declaration of Independence . . . oh look—"

"What?"

"New memoryware is on sale for tonight only."

"Come on, Ethan," said the second soldier. "It's getting dark. Let's just shoot 'em."

"Future president James Monroe is here. . . ." read Samantha.

The third soldier cocked his rifle.

"Alexander Hamilton, too. . . ."

"I never thought I would say this," said Fred. "But boy do I miss Sam."

FOUR

I knew we were goners. If only Sam had time warped with us. He would have known something smart to save us. This was the end of the Time Warp Trio.

"Ah, here it is," said Samantha. "Hessian troop strength." She read off her glasses. "Colonel Rall is in Trenton with fifteen hundred Hessians. Von Donop has another two thousand in Bordentown. And oh my—look at those British troops. Very interesting."

The lead soldier lowered his rifle. I started breathing again. "You know the location of the enemy troops?"

"Oh yeah," said Samantha. "And"—she tapped her glasses—"I also programmed in the school lunch menu for the rest of the year."

"Let me see that," said the leader. He tried on

Samantha's glasses. "I don't see nothing."

"Of course not," said Samantha. "Only I can access my files. And only I can show them to General Washington." She took her glasses back. "So what are we waiting for? Let's go see George."

The soldiers weren't sure. But you could tell they were impressed by Samantha's facts . . . and her gadgets.

"Get going up there to that house," said the lead soldier. He pointed up the hill with his rifle. "The generals are meeting just now."

Fred was so thrilled he smacked Samantha on the back. "Nice work."

Samantha smiled.

We started kicking our way through the ankle-deep snow. I couldn't believe we were going to actually meet the guy whose picture you see every day on the one-dollar bill. The father of our country. George Washington.

"And this better not be no spy hogwash," said the second soldier. "Or I'll hang you up on that tree myself."

Fred, Samantha, and I looked at the spooky black outline of a tree against the darkening sky. I was thinking about hanging—and rope tricks to get out of hanging—when I heard the noise.

It came from across the river. It sounded kind of animal, kind of mechanical, and kind of broken. Like a bad recording playing on a bad stereo.

"What the heck is that?" said Fred. "It sounds like a cat caught in a cement mixer."

MEOWWwwwrrkkKKKK, came the sound again.

"Rivets!" Samantha yelled. And you know how you always read about someone "jumping up and down"? That's exactly what Samantha did. She started jumping up and down. "Rivets, my kitty. Here, Rivets. Come to Mama."

On the other side of the river, we could see a strange catlike thing. It made a clanking sound and blinked a red light.

"That's not a cat," said Fred. "It's a clanking robot thing."

"Don't say that," said Samantha. "She's very sensitive." Samantha tapped her glasses. "Okay, now I've turned on the homing signal, which will bring her to me."

Across the river, the cat robot blinked its red light again. It kind of whistled *MEOWWwwrrkkKK*. Then it started walking along the river. Away from us.

"Oh no," said Samantha. "Stupid bargain sale bioware. Rivets, come back! That's the wrong way. You're headed for the Hessians."

We started to follow her, but we were all quickly stopped by the crossed rifles of Johnny Stark's men.

"We'll be right back," I said. "We just have to help our friend get her cat and a certain book."

All three soldiers cocked their rifles. They weren't buying it. "The only place you spies are going is to see the general."

Rivets walked downriver blinking, clanking, and sort of meowing.

We walked upriver—toward George Washington, but away from our chance to find *The Book* and get safely home.

FIVE

We found ourselves standing in the doorway to a small dining room. The room was filled with guys in uniforms. There must have been fifteen of them. They looked important. But they also looked pretty gloomy for a bunch of guys who were about to launch a surprise attack to save their new country.

Everyone looked up at us.

Our New Hampshire guard saluted and said, "Sir, we found these three outside. Sorry to interrupt, but they say they have important information about the enemy troops. Matter of life and death, they say."

"Thank you, soldier," said a young general with long brown hair. "But we won't be needing any more information. General Washington has called off all plans."

"Should we take them back outside and hang them?" said our guard.

"What?" said Samantha.

"I said, 'Should we take you back outside—'"

"No, not you," said Samantha, pushing past the guard. "General Washington? Not crossing the Delaware? This can't be true. It will mess up everything. He has to surprise the Hessian troops at Trenton."

"That's exactly what I said," said a general with a deep voice.

"The men are sick," said another general.

"The weather is against us."

"The Hessians are professional soldiers. We can't match them."

"But if we don't strike now, we may never have another chance."

"I say we can do it."

All the generals around the table started talking at the same time. They completely forgot about us. Someone banged on the table to make his point. The arguing got louder and louder until—

"Gentlemen!" came a voice from the doorway opposite us. "Gentlemen," said a tall man in a blue and silver coat.

Everyone went quiet.

That's when I figured out who it was. His face looked a little skinnier than the face in the picture we usually see. But there was no doubt about it. The tall man standing in the doorway was George Washington.

The man on the one-dollar bill spoke again. "General Greene, what's all the commotion?"

The general with the brown hair looked at us, then back at George Washington. "General Washington, sir. We have new information about the British and Hessian troops. Some of us still think we should go through with your surprise attack plan."

Half of the officers at the dining room table nodded their heads. The other half didn't look so sure.

A short fat guy with a seriously thick Scottish accent spoke up. "That's a bit of nonsense. All we've got is three wee lads telling us they have news to sell." The fat general pointed at us. "And for all we know, they are liars."

I don't know what got Samantha madder— being called a liar or a wee lad. Whichever it was, it launched her into action.

24

"Oh, but you have to cross the Delaware," said Samantha. "This is your chance to take the Hessians by surprise, turn the war around, save the United States of America, and save my cat."

"Whaaaa?" said General Washington.

"You had them with us," I said. "Right up until the bit about your cat."

Everyone started arguing again.

"Gentlemen," said George Washington. "Our army is tired and sick and hungry. Most of the men are ready to leave when their enlistments are up next week. What information can change that?"

The man on the one-dollar bill looked at Samantha and Fred and me.

Everyone in the room looked at us.

SIX

Everyone was still looking at us.

"Well," I said. "Think of Americans two hundred years from now. We will sure be glad . . . I mean they will sure be glad you fought for them."

"Yeah," said Fred. "It would be terrible if you didn't win the war and keep our country going. Can you imagine no more New York? No more New York pizza? No more New York Yankees?"

We got nothing but a lot of blank looks.

And I think we would have been swinging from the wrong end of a rope by the banks of the Delaware River if Samantha hadn't jumped into action.

"Okay, here's the plan for the shoot," said Samantha. "I'm going to need lots of action, lots of energy. I also need a big piece of paper and a pencil."

The roomful of generals all looked left, right, under their chairs.

"Nobody brought pencil or paper?" said Samantha.

"It's a secret meeting," said the general next to her.

"Fred, you help me." Samantha took a long half-burned stick out of the fireplace and handed it to Fred. She moved a vase off a side table to clear a blank piece of wall.

"General Washington," said Samantha. (She had to look up to talk to him. You'd never know it from the dollar bill, but he is a tall guy.) "Here are your plans. . . ." She tapped her glasses. "Right here."

General Washington looked too freaked out to say anything.

"Watch this." Samantha clicked her glasses on. They shot a beam of light like a projector on the wall.

General Washington jerked back a little in surprise, then he leaned in closer to read the display.

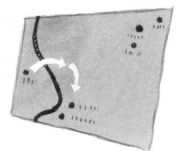

"Tofu burgers and Tater Tots? What does this mean?"

"Uh no, wait. Not that. Just a second now."

Samantha flashed homework questions, a message to Joanie, a picture of Rivets on the wall.

The generals started to grumble.

"Do not be alarmed," I told them. "These are all just some of our, um . . . latest spy missions. Very top secret."

"There. Yes," said Samantha, just in time. A list of names and numbers and army symbols filled the wall.

Washington read them carefully, talking to himself. "Yes . . . fifteen hundred Hessians in Trenton. Plus two thousand more in Bordentown under von Donop . . . just as I had thought . . . British in Perth Amboy? New Brunswick? Princeton? Yes, if this were the case . . ."

Washington stepped back and looked at Samantha. "You know these numbers to be true?"

"I would bet the fate of our country on it," said Samantha. "And look." Samantha clicked her glasses again and projected a map on the wall.

"Fred, trace over this map with the charcoal end of the stick so everyone can see."

Fred, who is always pretty amazing at drawing, drew the best drawing of his life. It looked something like this:

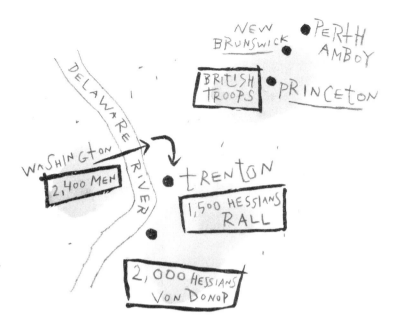

All of the generals crowded around to look.

"I get it," said Fred. And he explained as he drew. "The Hessians are here and here. The British troops are way back here, closer to New York, too far away to help. You cross here with twenty-four hundred troops. Your two other armies cross down here. You cross at night to keep it a secret. Nobody will expect an attack the day after Christmas. You surprise the Hessians, freak out the British, and save the country."

"And my report and my cat," said Samantha.

Everyone started pointing to Fred's map and talking all at once again.

"We have to try."

"Now or never."

"Can't be done," said the fat general.

Samantha gave him a look. Then she turned to General Washington. "Well? What do you say? Do we cross the Delaware and get this show started?"

"Hmmm," said George Washington.

"Or if not," I said. "Have you seen a blue book with silver designs?"

SEVEN

Washington held his chin and stared at the map on the wall.

"This is exactly how I imagined it. I attack with a division from the north. Ewing attacks from the south. Cadwalader pins the other Hessians at Bordentown."

It seemed like everyone in that small dining room held their breath while Washington talked to himself.

"The British troops are too far away to be any help to the Hessians. The boats are ready. This could be our last chance." Washington looked from the map to all of his generals gathered in the room. "We will attack. We cross the Delaware tomorrow night. Our watchword will be 'Victory or Death.'"

The room went nuts. We whooped and shouted. The generals whooped and shouted. Well, most of them did. The small fat guy gave Samantha and Fred and me a mean look. He was not happy we had wrecked his plans for Christmas.

Samantha snapped more vids. "Fantastic. Great action. I hope this works."

Fred and I stopped cheering.

"What do you mean, 'hope this works'?" I said. "I thought we were done. Washington crosses the Delaware. He surprises the Hessians. America wins the Revolutionary War. It's history, right?"

Samantha pushed her glasses up on her nose. "Well, not exactly. Us being here could change things."

"Yeah," said Fred. "Like we changed things for the good already. Didn't you hear the general? They're going to attack."

"Yes," said Samantha. "But it's like the ONE UNBENDING TIME WARP RULE says."

Fred and I must have looked a bit blank.

"You do know the ONE UNBENDING TIME WARP RULE, don't you?" said Samantha. "Don't tell me you haven't read at least that much of *The Book*."

"Oh, we know that," I said.

"Totally," said Fred. "Obviously. Of course we know that. Who doesn't?"

Samantha looked at us and shook her head.

"The ONE UNBENDING TIME WARP RULE is: *Haud finitum nisi finitum.*"

"Right," I said.

"Totally," said Fred.

"In English that means, *It ain't over till it's over.*"

"Got it," I said.

"Totally," said Fred.

"Sooo the whole Victory or Death thing could still go either way," I said, thinking out loud. "We could get the Victory. We could get the Death."

"Exactly," said Samantha.

I thought about that for just a second. That's all it took. "We have got to get out of here—right now."

"Yeah, but how?" said Fred.

"Here's our plan of attack," I said. "We go find that stupid cat—"

"She's not stupid. She's an Artificial Intelligence Lifeform," said Samantha.

"We go find that stupid Artificial Intelligence Lifeform," I said. "Follow it to *The Book*. And we warp out of here before all of the Victory or Death. Good plan? Yes. Come on."

I dragged Samantha and Fred over to General Washington. I shook George Washington's hand. (I figured a guy doesn't get too many chances to do that in a lifetime.)

"Thank you, Mr. General Washington, sir. It was very nice meeting you. Congratulations on the attack. Good luck with the rest of the war. I know you'll make us a great country."

General Washington shook my hand. "Thank you all for your valuable information." He took some silver coins out of his coat. "Here is your payment."

"Oh, we don't want money," said Samantha.

"Some of us might want money," said Fred.

"We were just glad to help," I said. This was going easier than I had expected. "Now, if you will excuse us, we have to go find a cat and catch a *Book* out of here."

Washington nodded. "Yes, you've been a great help. But no one may leave. We cannot risk losing the element of surprise."

"Oh, we won't tell anyone," I said. "I won't even tell Sam if you don't want me to."

Washington called over the New Hampshire guys. "We have much work to do. Any attempt to escape will be punished by instant death."

And he seemed like such a nice guy on the dollar bill.

"Understood?" said General George Washington.

"Yes sir!" said the New Hampshire guys.

"Yes sir," said Samantha.

"Yes sir," said Fred.

I saw our last chance to warp safely out of there disappear. I didn't know what else to say but, "Yes sir."

The rest of the night was a crazy blur of maps and plans and details. Fred, hungry as always, found us some bread and cider. Our guards found us a corner with a straw mattress to sleep on.

So that's how I spent Christmas Eve, dreaming not of Santa Claus but of squeezing that stupid cat until it gave up *The Book, The Book, The Book.* . . .

EIGHT

Christmas Day started gray and not at all sunny. There was snow on the ground, a light wind in the trees, and two thousand four hundred men marching down to cross the Delaware River.

It was nuts.

It looked like ten all-school assemblies and twenty lunchroom crowds smashed together.

"Whoa," said Fred. "You have got to be kidding. Washington is going to move all of these guys across the river?"

Ethan, our guard, nodded his head. "Yep. And two hundred horses, every man with food for three days, and every cannon we got."

Fred, Samantha, and I looked at the crazy mob up and down the river and around the dock. Men and horses swarmed around the ferry house. A few of the generals and other officers stood out in their uniforms and three-cornered hats. The rest of the soldiers wore all different kinds of outfits—hunting shirts, coats, shoulder belts, rags, and wraps.

A round man with a booming voice shouted orders at the men loading cannons on the boats.

"That's Colonel Knox," said Ethan. "He's in charge of the artillery. I hear the army started with three hundred cannons up in New York. That eighteen or so right there is all that's left."

A crowd of men wrestled the cannons onto giant black boats on the river. The boats were each as big as a school bus.

A loose cannonball dropped into a boat with a loud *thunk*. A short guy directing the boats started yelling at Colonel Knox.

"And that would be Colonel Glover," said Ethan. He gave a laugh. "I wouldn't mess with him. He's in charge of all the Massachusetts fisherman. They're the ones who know what they're doing with boats."

"Amazing," said Samantha. She was going crazy snapping vids of men, horses, cannons, flags, guys no older than us with drums and flutes. "Who is that? What are those?"

Ethan kept us under guard. And he kept describing everything for Samantha's report.

"Those boys there are the Third Regiment of

37

CLICK

CLICK

Virginia. Some of General Washington's favorites, 'cause he's from Virginia."

Dark clouds rolled overhead. A wet snow started to fall.

"That's the Maryland Rifles, Connecticut Troopers, Second and Third New Hampshire, First Pennsylvania Rifles."

"Those guys don't have any shoes," said Fred.

"Rhode Island boys," said Ethan. "They are tough."

Men streamed down to the ferry all day. Knox and his men didn't finish loading the cannons on the big black boats until late afternoon. By then the snow had turned to sleet and rain.

We saw General Washington everywhere. He cheered on his men down at the docks. He talked to the men waiting in ranks up and down the shore. He spoke to messengers riding in and out of the crowd on horses. He ducked inside the ferry house.

Fred and I shivered under the small protection of a tree. Samantha and Ethan didn't seem to notice the driving cold sleet and rain.

"I thought this was Washington Crossing the Delaware," said Fred. "Not Washington and His Guys Standing Around Freezing Their Butts Off."

Ethan, our guard, leaned on his rifle, calm as ever. "Can't cross nothing until dark," he said. "We'd be sitting ducks if any Hessians spotted us."

The rain and snow came down harder.

"They'd have to be crazy to be out in weather like this," I said.

"Like us," said Fred.

Samantha adjusted her glasses. Somehow she was still completely warm and dry. She saw me staring at her silver coat. "Therm Fabric," she said. "It repels rain, snow, cold, and wind. And I've patched the controls into my glasses, too."

"Good for you," I said. "I'm freezing."

"Do you want to trade coats for a while?" said Samantha.

The silver fabric looked pretty cool.

"A girl's coat?" I said. "No way."

I went back to freezing.

Fred slapped his arms around his body. He pulled his hat low. "Enough is enough. This is Christmas. I'm supposed to be home opening my new NFL Street game."

"Hey yeah," I said. "I was going to get Killer Krazed Racer."

Fred started walking.

"Stop," said Ethan. "I'll have to shoot if you try to escape."

Fred kept walking. "I'm not escaping. I just remembered something I have to tell General Washington."

Fred disappeared into the crowd of men around the ferry house. Ten minutes later he was on the dock with General Washington, waving us down.

Samantha and Ethan and I worked our way through the crowd at the water's edge. We shuffled across a ramp from the dock to a boat and packed in with a mess of generals and soldiers.

"What did you say?" I asked Fred.

"I told him we had new information that no enemy troops were anywhere near us. And that now would be a safe time to cross."

"But we don't know that," said Samantha.

"Hey he's the one who said, 'I cannot tell a lie.' Not me," said Fred.

"I don't know how history has survived you guys," said Samantha.

Big flat floating chunks of ice banged off the side of the boat. The Massachusetts fishermen held us steady.

Things looked pretty grim. The boat loading was taking too long. The weather was working against us. The ice in the river could wreck the whole attack.

Washington stepped into the boat. You could see that every man looked to him. Everyone wondered what he was thinking. Would he keep going with the crossing and the attack?

Washington poked the round, loud artillery guy Colonel Knox with the toe of his boot. "Move that fat butt of yours, Henry . . . but move it slowly or you'll swamp us all."

Colonel Knox laughed.

The Massachusetts boat guys laughed.

The men waiting on the docks started laughing and retelling Washington's crack.

It was cold and wet and dark and icy. It was

going to take some kind of miracle for Fred and me to get back safely home and open our Christmas presents. But George Washington was going to get his men safely across, and carry on with the plan.

NINE

So I have to tell you, the real George Washington crossing the Delaware scene looked nothing like the painting.

For one—it was completely dark and cold and raining, sleeting, and snowing.

Two—the boat was way bigger than that dinky thing in the painting.

Three—none of us, except the guys poling and steering the boat, were standing up.

Four—there weren't any pretty white icebergs sticking out of the water. There were nasty flat slabs of black ice thunking into the side of the boat, each one sounding like it was going to sink us.

Five—we weren't flying any flags.

And six—they forgot to put me and Fred and Samantha in the painting.

I know Fred and I were ducked down, trying to

stay warm. But you couldn't miss Samantha in her silver Therm Fabric coat, directing the whole operation for her history project.

We did get across. And so did the rest of the soldiers—boat by boat by boat. All two thousand four hundred of them. And two hundred horses. And eighteen cannons.

By the time the whole army was across, it was three o'clock in the morning.

General Washington stood out in the freezing rain. "If my men are going to be outside in this nasty weather without shelter, so am I," he said.

The last boat filled with cannons and ammunition unloaded.

"All right," said Fred. "We crossed the Delaware. Now let's get that *Book* and warp out of here."

"Uh, Fred," said Samantha. "You're forgetting one small detail."

"I know, I know," said Fred. "*It ain't over till it's over.* So where are the Hessians? Let's get this over."

Samantha checked the directions in her glasses. "Well, Trenton and the Hessians are that way." She pointed south. "About . . . nine miles."

Fred froze. "Nine miles? Are you crazy? Are we

crazy? Whose idea was it to hike nine miles in the cold? In the dark? In the freezing rain?"

The wind suddenly gusted, blowing the rain and snow sideways, stinging our faces.

"Company! Fall in!" shouted one of the officers.

The command was echoed up and down the ranks of two thousand four hundred wet men.

"Fall in!"

Another gust of freezing rain.

"Fall in!"

Mud squished beneath our feet.

We fell in line with the rest of the guys from the First New Hampshire Regiment.

Mud and rain splattered everywhere. Mud and rain splattered everyone—everyone except Samantha. That future fiber coat of hers kept her clean and warm and dry.

Fred and I were now cold, muddy, soaked, and miserable.

Samantha didn't seem to notice. She talked into her bracelet.

"Four o'clock in the morning. Only two hours until dawn. Under good conditions, troops can cover three miles in an hour. Our American soldiers, already tired and cold and loaded with gear, will be lucky to cover two miles in an hour."

Samantha recorded the rain pelting down, the squish of the mud.

"General Washington knows that his army will never make it to Trenton in time for a surprise attack at dawn. What will he do now?"

Then, almost like he was answering the question, General Washington rode up on his horse. "Forward, men," he called out. "Stay by your officers. Forward! March!"

We marched.

And we marched.

And we marched some more.

"Nice roads," said Fred.

We were supposed to be on a road. But all of the men and horses and wagons had turned the dirt road into a muddy ditch.

We marched so long men fell asleep on their feet. Soldiers stumbled. Horses fell. Soon mud caked everyone's boots, clothes, and hair.

"What's with the red tracks in the snow?" said Fred. "Is that some kind of trail marker?"

"That's blood," said the soldier next to Fred. "From the boys with no boots."

"Yikes," said Samantha.

"Yuck," said Fred.

The rain slashed sideways.

The soldier next to me tucked his gun under his arm, trying to keep it dry.

"Bad news," said the soldier next to him. "Everybody's powder is wet. I'll bet there's not a gun in the whole company that will fire now."

"Maybe it isn't such a good idea to fight, then," said Samantha.

The muddy longhaired soldier next to me nodded. "And these Hessians are no joke. They're paid to fight. And they're the best in the world."

"Do you think we could maybe talk them out of the Trenton attack?" said Samantha.

"I'll bet you could," said Fred

Johnny Stark heard his men. "I like the chances of our boys even if our guns won't fire. We'll use our rifles to knock heads if we have to!"

The men cheered and picked up their step.

"Oh well," said Samantha. She checked her glasses. They glowed red. "At least we're on the right track. Rivets is straight ahead."

"Lucky us," I said, freezing rain dripping off my nose. "When we catch up with that bucket of bolts, I'm going to—"

"Be nice," said Samantha. "It's not her fault she leaks sometimes."

We slogged through the muddy slush.

I was glad we were headed toward *The Book*. I was not too glad we were headed toward the best soldiers in the world . . . or that we had guns that wouldn't fire.

We marched.

And we marched.

And we marched some more.

Then, after what seemed like forever, we stopped. Through the drifting morning mist, we could see the edge of a village.

"Eight o'clock in the morning. The day after Christmas. Seventeen seventy-six," Samantha whispered into her bracelet. "General George Washington and his army stand just outside Trenton."

TEN

Fred, Samantha, and I . . . and the army of General Washington . . . stood just outside Trenton. I turned to look back—and saw a shocking sight.

I don't know what I was expecting to see. Maybe a bunch of army guys in neat rows like you always see in the movies. But that's not what I saw when I turned around.

I saw a wild, crazy-looking mob of men. A huge crowd of rifles, hats, arms, legs, long stringy hair— all caked in layers of mud as far as I could see. Horse and men steaming in the cold mist. Metal clanking. Feet stomping. Steam rising.

It didn't look like an army. It looked a hundred times scarier than any army. It looked like a huge gang of wildman mud monsters of the woods, ready to take on anything in their way.

Straight ahead of us, General Washington and two other officers on horses stood talking to a farmer carrying an armload of firewood.

Samantha checked her glasses. They gave a little red glow.

"Rivets," she whispered. "Straight ahead."

"That figures," said Fred. I turned to look at Fred and almost jumped back. Covered from head to toe in mud, he looked as crazy as the rest of the army. He looked at me and bugged his eyes out, too.

"You look like a walking pig pen," I said.

"Just like you," said Fred.

I wiped mud off my leg and splatted it on Fred.

"An Abominable Mud Man."

"Just like you."

Fred wiped a handful of mud off his coat and splatted it on me.

"Frankenmud."

"Just like you."

Fred scooped up a handful of mud to splatter Samantha.

"Hey, where is Samantha?"

I looked all around. She was gone.

"There," said Fred. He pointed toward George Washington and the farmer.

Samantha was following the red dot of her cat tracker. "Rivets," she said. She had no idea where she was walking.

RiVetſ...

"She's going to get run over in the attack," said Fred.

"Sam will never forgive us if we lose his great-granddaughter," I said. "We've got to get her."

We slipped and slid and dodged our way around muddy soldiers. We were almost up to Washington and his officers.

"Where is the Hessian guard?" we heard Washington asking the farmer.

The man pointed to a figure leaning against the house. "He's right there. Asleep. I walked right past him. They were up late last night celebrating

Christmas. The other ten of them on guard are asleep inside."

"Rivets," said Samantha.

"If we can surround the house and silence the guard," said Washington, "it would be very much to our advantage."

And just like that, the attack began.

The two officers thought Washington was giving them orders to attack. They drew their swords and charged the house. They knocked down the single guard, ran over the Hessians' stacked muskets, jumped off their horses, and smashed in the door of the house.

General Washington turned his horse to face the waiting army. I don't know if he had wanted them to attack. But it was too late to stop now.

"Forward men! Everyone attack! Attack!"

Fred and I grabbed Samantha. We turned just in time to see the whole crazy mud-covered sleet-mad army whooping and charging toward us.

"Run!" I yelled.

And the three of us ran ahead of the attack to keep from getting trampled.

Howling, screaming, cursing, mad mudmen and horses thundered out of the mist.

Washington called for his troops to divide into two columns. They split and swarmed toward the town of Trenton. A few shots rang out from the house. Men raced over the fields and fences yelling, screaming, and waving their guns.

Three of the Hessians who had been in the house crawled out a back window and ran toward town.

General Knox and his men rolled cannons forward and boomed a few shots after them.

Johnny Stark charged up on his horse. "Come on now all you Vermont and New Hampshire men! Let's not leave the whole battle to the Virginians!"

And if anybody was still asleep in Trenton, the screeching whoop of Johnny Stark and his crazy New Englanders woke them up for sure.

It also snapped Samantha out of her cat tracking trance. "We're attacking."

"No kidding," said Fred. "Did your glasses tell you that?"

"Forward!" yelled Ethan and the rest of the New Hampshire guys.

"Okay!" I yelled back.

And we dove into the mad charge of hundreds of men and horses sweeping past on either side of us.

We charged into the streets of Trenton. Hessian

troops ran out of buildings. Hessian cavalry guys jumped on their horses and rode back and forth. A few muskets banged and fired here and there, but no one got hit. The soldiers were right—the rain and snow had made the muskets too wet to fire. The cannon powder stayed dry inside the can-nons.

Johnny Stark led his men, and us, toward the middle of the town.

The Hessians tried to form lines in the street, but were run over by our howling mud soldiers.

I spotted more Hessians at the end of the street. They rolled out two of their shiny brass cannons, the only thing left that would fire in the rain.

A cannon blast from the other end of the street boomed. It knocked the Hessian cannons sideways. It was the other column of Washington's men.

Left and right, Hessian soldiers dropped their guns and surrendered.

One last big group of Hessian soldiers ran out of town, followed by our still howling mud-covered guys. The Hessians made a break to try to escape across a bridge. But Colonel Glover and his Massachusetts fisherman were already there, blocking the way with three cannons.

The Hessian soldiers, trapped in the middle of a

field, formed a three-sided square and faced the American enemy surrounding them. The Hessian general jumped on his horse. He gathered his men for one last charge.

I saw General Washington, sitting high in the saddle of a white horse. He called for his men to get ready.

Then a single shot rang out. It knocked the Hessian general to the ground.

There was no charge.

The Hessian soldiers lowered their flags as a sign of surrender. The Hessian officers presented their swords handle-first to an American officer.

The Battle of Trenton was over.

George Washington and his tired, wet, ragged band of mudmen had defeated the best soldiers in the world.

ELEVEN

Fred, Samantha, and I sat at a wooden table in a stone house in the middle of Trenton. A warm, bright fire burned in the fireplace. It had only been an hour and a half since the attack started, but it was over.

Samantha had followed her cat tracker, and it had actually worked. Rivets, the spazzy robo-cat was curled up right next to the fire, just like it had been waiting for us.

There was only one small . . . well, one big problem. We had found Rivets all right. But Rivets hadn't found *The Book*. It was nowhere inside. Nowhere in the drizzly outside.

"Stupid cat," said Fred.

"Stupid cat," I said.

"She is not," said Samantha, fiddling with her glasses. "There must be a bug in the Seek program. *The Book* has to be around here somewhere."

Rivets didn't seem to care one way or the other. It gave one of its bad *MEEOowwwrrrkkkkkk* sounds and jumped up on Samantha's lap. Or it tried to jump up on Samantha's lap. It miscalculated, sailed over Samantha's lap, and crashed into the stone fireplace with a *clank*.

Mee—OWWWW. ME—OWWWWW.

"Stupid cat," I said.

"Stupid cat," said Fred.

Samantha fiddled with her glasses some more.

Ethan stood in the doorway. "Well, I'm glad we didn't hang you right away after all. Crazy as it was, the surprise attack worked out pretty near perfect."

Out the window we could see groups of Hessian prisoners being marched off. Some were still in their nightshirts. Our soldiers covered the streets of Trenton cheering.

"We got us nearly a thousand Hessian prisoners, six cannons, ammunition wagons, and the flags of three Hessian regiments."

"That's great," said Fred. "You didn't happen to also get a thin blue *Book* with silver markings did you?"

"What?" said Ethan.

"Oh, don't mind him," said Samantha. "He just gets grumpy when he doesn't get to eat . . . every hour."

"I do not," grumped Fred. "But hey, do you have anything to eat?"

Ethan handed Fred a biscuit out of his pack. Fred chomped on it like a starving wild mud animal. He barely made a dent in it.

"Yow," said Fred. "Are you sure this isn't a rock you picked up by accident?"

"Army chow," said Ethan. "It's easier if you use your back teeth."

Fred gnawed away at the biscuit.

Samantha held her glasses up to the light. "I'm sure it's working. And look at this fantastic report. It's all there. The meeting at Decision House. Gathering at the ferry. Night crossing. The march, the march, the

61

march . . . okay maybe I should edit out some of that . . . the charge. And—victory."

"Mrrrmmph," said Fred, with a mouthful of rock biscuit.

"Okay," said Ethan. "We're heading out. Y'all are free citizens again. Free to go where you please." He gave us a salute, and disappeared out the door.

"But—" I started to say.

"But what?" said Samantha.

Rivets jumped up into Samantha's lap. This time it made it.

I was suddenly very tired and muddy and hungry . . . and wanting very much to go home.

"But how are we supposed to find *The Book* and not get stuck here in seventeen seventy-six for the rest of our lives?"

"Mmrrrmph," agreed Fred.

Samantha rechecked her glasses. "I swear it's working."

TWELVE

I stood up and grabbed Samantha's glasses. I was just about to whack her on the head with them, when I heard horses ride up to the house.

"Where are they?" boomed a familiar voice.

General George Washington, all six-feet-plus large of him, walked into the room. Two officers stood with him.

"There you are," said our man on the dollar bill.

For a guy who had just pulled off an amazing surprise attack that would change the course of the Revolutionary War and start the country that would become the United States of America, General Washington did not look very happy.

"We didn't do it," said Fred.

"I can explain," I said, gently putting Samantha's glasses back on her.

The glasses started blinking.

Rivets started blinking and making a sound like a

purr mixed with handful of paperclips being ground in an electric pencil sharpener.

General Washington took off his hat. He looked tired.

"We have won an important battle here. I wanted to thank you for your information." He looked at Samantha. "And for reminding me to follow my instincts and what I knew was right."

Fred coughed down the last of his biscuit.

"Oh, no problem," said Fred. "Glad I could help."

"It was all your plan, and all your doing, General Washington," said Samantha. "Thank you for helping out with my report."

General Washington frowned. "I've just learned that neither of my other armies managed to cross the river. We must head back to Pennsylvania immediately." He looked lost in thought for a minute. "We were also very lucky. Now we have horses, ammunition, food, clothing, medicine. But most importantly—we have won the chance to continue our fight."

We all stared at General George Washington. He really was a giant of a man.

Rivets purred, blinked, clanked.

General Washington handed a wrapped present to Samantha.

"Merry Christmas," he said.

He saluted. The officers saluted. Then they were gone.

The fire crackled.

Rivets purr-clanked like mad, then suddenly blinked green.

"Ah, just as I thought," said Samantha. "What a nice man." She put the present in her lap next to Rivets. She took off her glasses and clicked them. "I just wish I could have gotten that on vid."

Fred wiped the crumbs off his mud-covered lap. "We're stuck in muddy seventeen seventy-six, and you're still worried about your report?"

Samantha looked up, and paused for effect.

"Oh, I don't think we'll be stuck for too long." She tore back a corner of the green wrapping. "Because I have a present that's blue . . ." She tore back a little more. "And silver . . ." She held it up. "And—"

"It's *The Book*!" yelled Fred.

"How? What? He?" I said.

I didn't know where to start asking all of the questions I had.

"Of course," said Samantha. "It's elementary time wormhole science, you see." She spun her glasses, trying to look cool.

And that's when Rivets jumped up, bit the glasses, and leaked all over Samantha's silver coat . . . and *The Book*.

A line of blue sparks jumped from Rivets's head to Samantha's glasses. I heard a pop, then the tear of metal claw on Therm Fabric, then the whoosh of green time-traveling mist.

"No," said Samantha, already swirled in green mist. "My report is erased!"

The green mist swirled warmly over Fred and me. We smiled.

"Bad cat," said Samantha.

Green mist covered our muddy bodies.

"Bad, bad cat," said Samantha.
Green mist covered our muddy heads.
"You are a very bad cat."
And we and Samantha and her stupid cat . . .
were time warp gone.

THIRTEEN

Fred threw his snowball.

I ducked behind a tree just in time.

Fred's snowball popped against the tree trunk.

We were back in Brooklyn. Back on the street in front of my house. Back the day before Christmas. Snowing like crazy. Vacation. Perfect.

"How weird was that?" said Fred, from behind his tree.

"Completely weird," I said. While I kept talking, I made a pile of snowball ammunition. "And it really wasn't our fault at all, for maybe the first time ever."

"I can't wait to tell Sam

what a goofball his great-grand-daughter is," said Fred. "Her homework ate her cat?"

"What a stupid cat," I said. I gathered up my six snowballs in my arms. I started sneaking around the parked cars covered with snow for my George Washington special surprise attack.

"That coat material was pretty cool, though," said Fred, still behind his tree.

I snuck closer.

"I mean did you see that stuff?" said Fred. "It looked like just any old regular coat, but everything bounced off it. How do you think it did that? Was it like an inside-out thermos?"

I was almost on him.

"Hey, Joe." Fred peeked around his tree. "I know you're going to try that lame trick where you throw one snowball up in the air, and then fire the other one. I'm not falling for it this time. Joe?"

Fred had no idea I was right behind him. I quietly raised my arm to unleash my surprise attack. Then we both heard an awful, frightening, terrible sound.

It came from somewhere behind me.

It sounded part animal, part mechanical.

It went, *MEoooowwwrrrrrkkkk.*

"Ahhhh!" I screamed.

"Ahhhh!" screamed Fred.

And Fred and I took off running, without looking back, to escape the surprise attack of you-know-what.

Tricks with
George Washington

General Washington crossed the Delaware River, surprised the Hessian troops, and went on to win independence for the new country of the United States of America. Did you know he can also turn into a mushroom? Here's how:

1. Take a U.S. one-dollar bill.

2. Fold it in half.

3. Fold about 3/4 of the bottom half back down until just the neck is showing. Now you have a George Washington Mushroom Head.